For Melanie and Joscelyne

Library of Congress Cataloging in Publication Number: 2016957831

ISBN: 978-1-68369-027-6

Printed in China

Typeset in Miller

Story and text by Jason Rekulak
Designed by Timothy O'Donnell
Special thanks to Chris Carter, Nicole Spiegel, and Josh Izzo
Production management by John J. McGurk

Quirk Books
215 Church Street
Philadelphia, PA 19106
quirkbooks.com

10 9 8 7 6 5 4 3 2

THE X FILES

EARTH CHILDREN ARE WEIRD

Based on characters created by Chris Carter

Illustrated by Kim Smith

QUIRK BOOKS

PHILADELPHIA

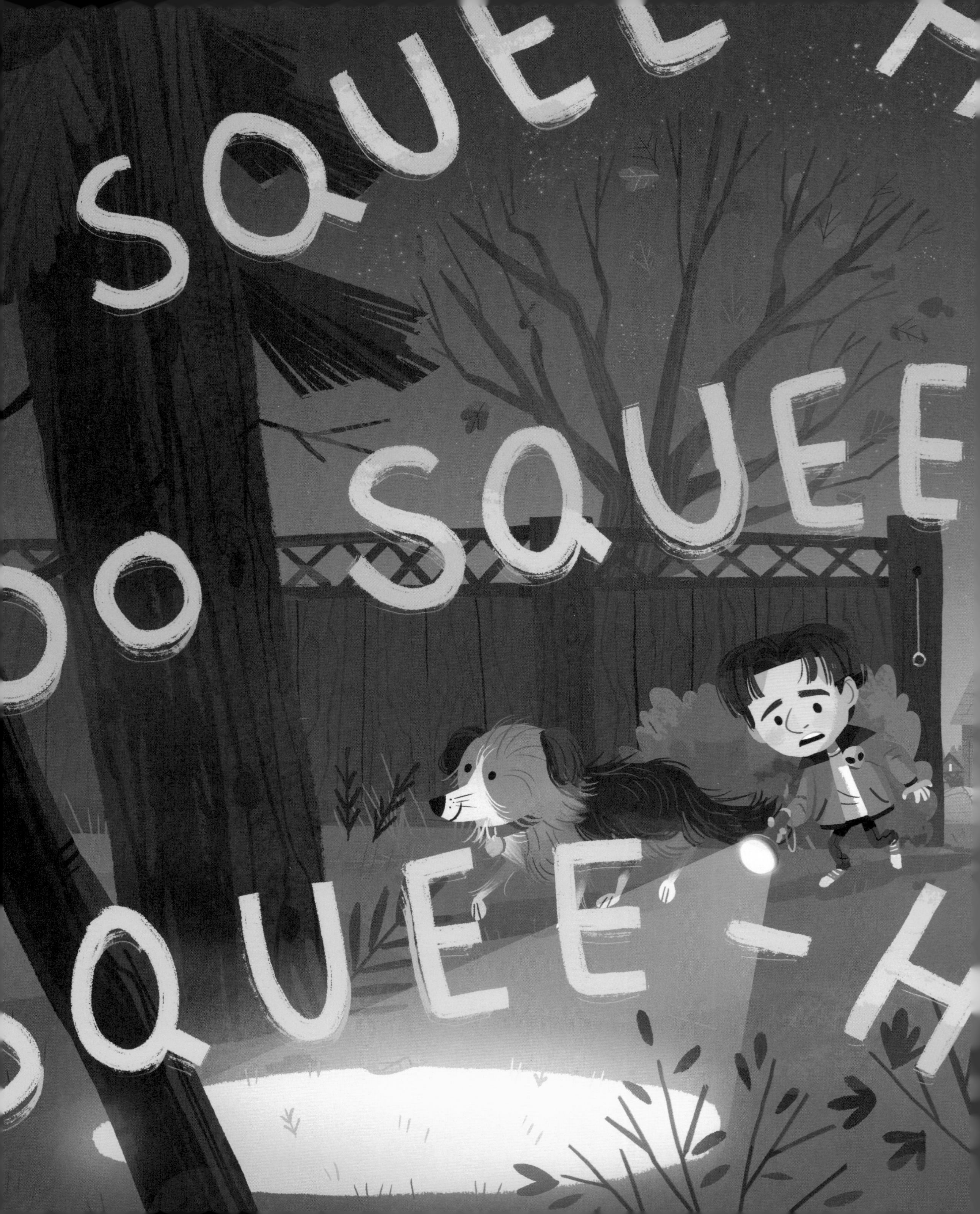

SQUEE
OO
SQUEE
QUEE-H

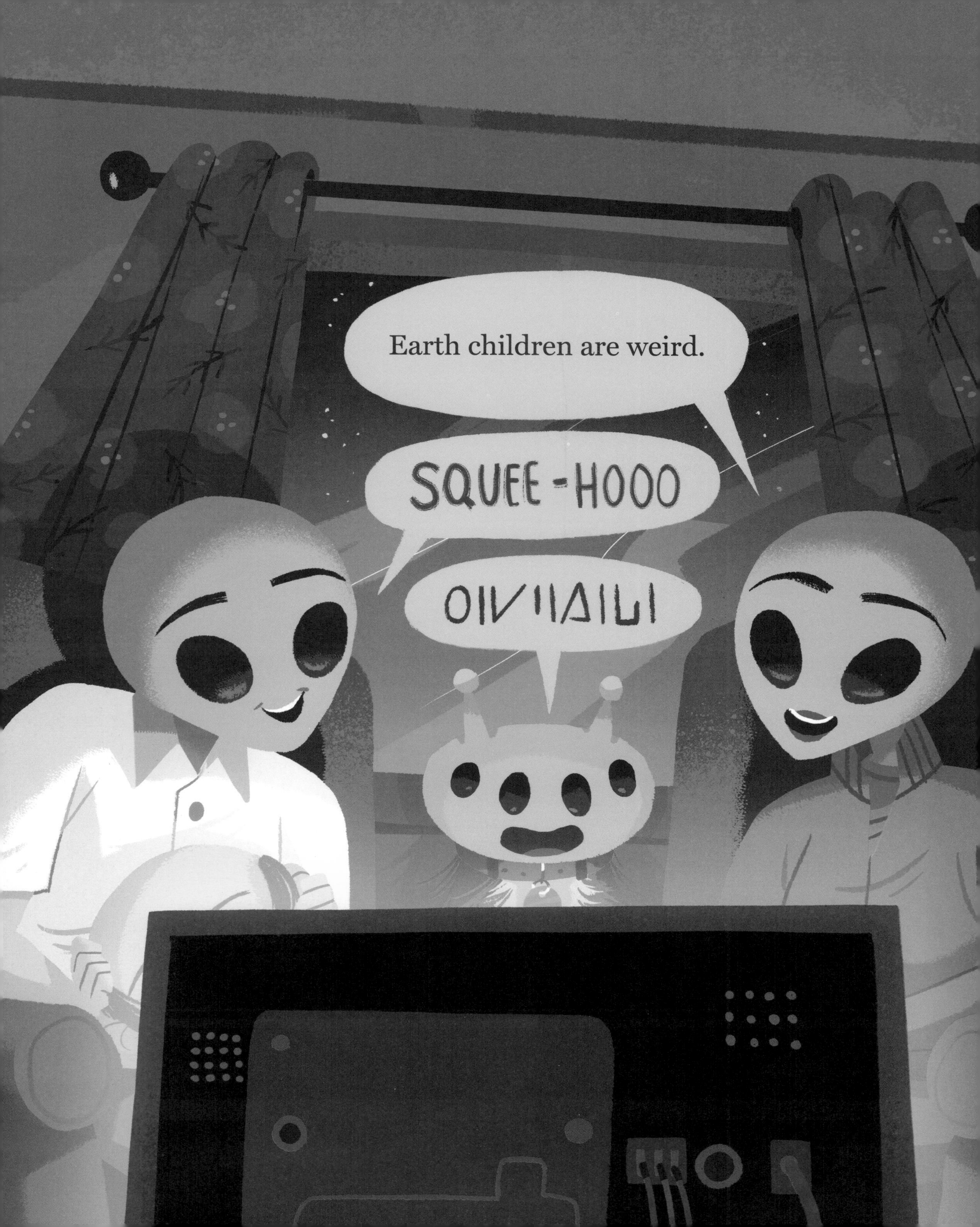
Earth children are weird.
SQUEE-HOOO